# Hiding Heidi

*For Martin*

SIMON AND SCHUSTER

First published in Great Britain in 2016 by Simon and Schuster UK Ltd • 1st Floor, 222 Gray's Inn Road, London WC1X 8HB • A CBS Company
Text and illustrations copyright © 2016 Fiona Woodcock • The right of Fiona Woodcock to be identified as the author and illustrator of this
work has been asserted by her in accordance with the Copyright, Designs and Patents Act, 1988 • All rights reserved, including the right
of reproduction in whole or in part in any form • A CIP catalogue record for this book is available from the British Library upon request
ISBN: 978-1-4711-4447-9 (HB) • ISBN: 978-1-4711-4448-6 (PB) • ISBN: 978-1-4711-4449-3 (eBook)
Printed in China • 10 9 8 7 6 5 4 3 2 1

# Hiding Heidi

*by Fiona Woodcock*

**SIMON AND SCHUSTER**
London  New York  Sydney  Toronto  New Delhi

Heidi has a special talent.
Can you guess what it is?
I bet you can.

Look!
She's doing it again!

Heidi can't help it.

Wherever she goes and
whatever she does –
it just happens.

Sometimes Heidi's friends join in.
They're quite good.

But not as good as Heidi.

No-one's as good at hiding as she is.

She's a natural.

One day, Heidi was hanging out with her friends.
'Let's have a space-hopper race!' said Freddie.
'No, let's have a roller-skate race!' said Katie.
'No, no, no, let's not have a race at all,' said Lizzie.
'Let's play on the climbing frame!'

They couldn't agree.

So in the end they all played hide and seek.

Which Heidi won.
Of course.

The next day it was Heidi's birthday.
All her friends came over for a party.
Everyone was having a fantastic time.

When the music stopped, Heidi giggled.
'Now can we play hide and seek?'

Heidi's friends searched for her high . . .

. . . and low.

But as we know, she's just too good.

Freddie, Katie and Lizzie couldn't find Heidi.
But they did find some scrummy sundaes.

It wasn't until the very end of Heidi's party
that her friends finally found her.
And that was much too late.

Now her party was over Heidi thought

and thought

and thought.

The next day Heidi and her friends were hanging out.
'Let's have a space-hopper race!' said Freddie.

'Yes, let's!' said Heidi quickly,
before anyone else could say a word.

So they did.

Freddie was brilliant at bouncing.

Then they had a roller-skate race. With ribbons!
Katie was sensational at skating.

Then they clambered on the climbing frame.
Lizzie was incredible at climbing.

'See?' said Heidi as they all relaxed later.
'We don't ALWAYS have to play hide and seek . . .

. . . do we?'